Tails of Wa

Spooky
The Adventures of a Ship's Cat in WWII

Story by *Diane Condon-Boutier*
Illustrations by *Elisabeth Gontier*

Spooky : The Adventures of a Ship's Cat in WWII

For my mom, who heard this story and encouraged me to share it with you...

« If history were told in the form of stories, it would never be forgotten. » Rudyard Kipling

I am Spooky. I am a cat. But not just any cat. I am a ship's cat. And not just any ship's cat: I am a ship's cat who went to war.

The year is 1942. Europe is at war with Nazi Germany. I work on board a British ship carrying *coastal landing craft* * It is a type of troop transport ship. And we're fighting for freedom.

Freedom is that thing that lets every man, woman, child and CAT live in safe conditions. No one can tell them how to eat, how to dress, what songs to sing or which books to read.

Freedom is a special thing, and it's worth fighting for.

*Flat bottomed boat which carries soldiers directly to the beach

4

I know, because I hear the stories told by the sailors and soldiers on the boat where I work. They talk to each other about a man named Adolph Hitler. He took away people's freedom in France, Holland, Belgium, and even in Germany where he is the Chancellor. He wants everyone to do exactly as he decides: to think like him. Worse yet, he orders his soldiers to hurt anyone who doesn't act the same way he does. Adolph Hitler wants to crush freedom. And that's a very bad thing, indeed.

So, I went to work like so many others from different countries around the world. We don't agree with the Nazis who follow Adolph Hitler. We are a team of Allies.

We have decided to stop Adolph Hitler so that freedom may once again spread through Europe. We want people to live in peace and safety. The difference is that I'm a cat, and a female. But that's not a problem, because I work hard just like the soldiers.

Yes, I have a job. I keep the men's food safe from vermin – that means mice, rats, or even birds – which can eat human food or *contaminate** it by leaving their waste behind in the food storage areas.

It's a hard job and sometimes it can be dangerous. Most of the seagulls who try to steal food through the

ship's *portholes** are much bigger than I am. They try to peck at me when I defend the food. They swoop down and cry out, flapping their wings, hitting me to chase me away. But I stand strong, hiss and spit at them. If they come too close, I swat them away with my paws. Those who do, find out that I'm very good at standing on my back paws and balancing.

*contaminate means to poison, usually food or water supplies
*a porthole is a window on a ship

Rats are dangerous too. Once, I tried to chase a rat away from the butter *vat**. He bit me when I swatted at him. My paw got infected and the ship's medic had to clean it with *mercurochrome**. That stung! Then he bandaged my paw and put me on a blanket in my *hammock**.

I was very sick. I had a fever and was too tired to eat. The men came to see me one by one. They tried to feed me bits of tuna or chicken. They stroked my head and scratched my chin. I love that. They wanted to make me feel better.

Now, I know how important my job is. If I hadn't chased away that rat, the one who bit me, he could have poisoned the food my soldier friends eat. They would get sick, too. Then they wouldn't be able to fight Adolph Hitler's soldiers. We work together as a team, helping each other. I am a part of that team: a small part, but now I know how much I count. I am proud of my job.

*a vat is a large container for storing food
*mercurochrome is a red liquid medicine for cleaning wounds
*a hammock is a hanging bed for sailors on a boat

In just a short time I was feeling much better and went back to roaming through the *gangways* of the ship searching in every hidden corner.

Each morning I hop out of my hammock at first bell and start out on the lower decks. I *inspect*** all the doors to the storage areas, checking to see if they are shut. If one of them is open, then I know that there might be an *intruder*** inside eating the food and poisoning it with waste. I especially like spending time in the *galley***.

But look over there! The door to the vegetable storeroom is open! I slip quietly through the opening and hide beneath a shelf.

Then I wait.

I must be very quiet. If I hear a noise, like paper rustling, or cans bumping into one another, then I know for certain an intruder is there.

*A gangway is a hallway on a ship
*to inspect means to look at something very closely and carefully
*an intruder is a stranger who shouldn't be somewhere, like a thief
*the galley is the kitchen on a ship

Loud noises come from around the corner. Thump! Thump! Then, a loud BANG!

It's time for me to attack whatever is in there.

I'm a little afraid, because whatever it is must be pretty big to make such loud noises.

I crouch and stalk, one paw at a time, to the corner of the shelf.

The intruder is very close.

One more step and I'll see who it is.

My fur stands on end and my tail twitches.

I'm ready to pounce at any second.

Ready...

Steady...

GO!

I rush around the corner and leap onto my back paws, claws on my forefeet out and ready to attack!

PSSSSTTTT!

I hiss at the intruder!

"What the...? Hey! Spooky!

It's just me, Cook!

Calm down little girl!"

Wait! It's just my friend dropping onions off the shelf into a big cooking pan. He's the one making all the noise! He's the one who opened the door.

Whew! All that excitement for nothing. I can relax. All is well. But, now I've frightened him with my vigorous attack so I wind between his feet, purring. He smiles and pats me on the head.

"You're a fierce little girl! That was awfully impressive!"

Even if it was a false alert, I've done my job.

As I make my way up to the main deck, I can see that there is some commotion today. We've pulled up to the dock in Portsmouth, in the south of England. There are lots of new soldiers climbing aboard, bringing guns and heavy boxes of *ammunition**. Something important is taking place. I can feel it.

I stand by the top of the *gangplank** at attention greeting the new soldiers. Most of them wear Canadian uniforms. They're a different color from the Royal Navy boys I'm used to. They have different accents when speaking, too! Still, most of them stoop over and give me a quick stroke on the back as they go by. The line of men is very long, stretching down the dock. Our ship is going to be full to the gills!

I can see a group of British Royal Commandos, too. And with them are some U.S. Rangers. What a surprise! They've got a different accent too. Some of them are from Texas!

"Hey there, puss! Aren't you a nice greeter! Hey Eddie! There's a cat on board! Awww! And a sweet girl she is, too."

*ammunition is extra bullets, cannon shells and grenades
*a gangplank is the ramp used by people to climb on board a ship

Once everyone is on board, we inch away from the *quay**. It's already late at night. The soldiers are sitting in small groups on the top deck. Soon, we're at sea. I wander through the men, enjoying a pat

here and there. They're talking amongst themselves.

No one is sleepy. I hear someone say we've got a few hours left before we reach the French coast.

Wait! What? We're going to France? That's where the enemy soldiers are! This means we're headed into battle!

I listen closely to the conversations, trying to figure out what's going on. When I hear some Canadians, I stop to pay attention.

*a quay is the dock where a ship ties up

"You know, this is the first time that any large group of Allied soldiers is attacking the Nazis on European soil! I'm awfully proud to be part of this, aren't you René?"

"I sure am. If we can wreck some of the defense bunkers the Germans have put up along the beach in Dieppe, then we'll know exactly how and where to attack when we launch a full out assault later on."

"So, you think this is a kind of trial run?" asks Robert.

"Yup, *Winston Churchill** wants to know more about the port defenses. That way he can decide where to attack occupied Europe. And it won't be long before more of the American Army shows up to lend a hand." explains René.

"What do you mean? There are already *Yanks** with us?"

"Yeah, but not very many. The Rangers who are here on board are training under the British Commandos. The Allied army is going to need a lot more well trained men if we're going to finish off the Nazis."

"Yeah, I guess you're right. The Nazis aren't going to just give up, are they?"

Both René and Robert stop talking. They look worried about the battle to come. I can understand why.

Goodness, this is a very important mission we're on. That adds a new twist to my job! These soldiers need to keep their spirits up. I know! I'll get them to play with me!

*Winston Churchill is the Prime Minister of Great Britain
*Yanks is a slang word meaning Americans from the 'Yankee Doodle' song

To start out the game, I choose a Ranger who's writing a letter. With my claws tucked in, I pounce on his hand. He's surprised, but laughs at me.

"Hey, kitty! You're messing up my handwriting! You want to play, don't you?

And that's how several of the soldiers end up on all fours chasing me around the deck. I swat their pencils and pull at the cords on their packs: anything to get their attention. The others watch us, laughing. This is what I wanted. They're going off to war where they'll have plenty of serious times ahead of them.

If I can help them have a little fun now, well that's just purrrfect.

When our *convoy* of ships comes close to the coast, the landing craft are lowered into the water. The soldiers begin to climb down inside. I make a big decision. They'll need my moral support during the dangerous hours ahead. So, I leap into the small boat.

"Oh, no you don't, kitty cat! You're not coming along!"

*convoy means a group of vehicles setting off together

Hands pass me from one soldier to the next until I'm back on the ship. But I am a stubborn cat. I'm waiting until everyone is in the landing craft and they cast off. Ok, looks like the last man is in. I flex the muscles of my back legs, swing my tail out and give a huge push off the deck. Woo-hoo! I'm flying! Almost as well as those nasty seagulls!

Landing isn't so great. The boat was farther away than I thought and I hit the bottom in a not very dignified tumble. It doesn't matter. I'm on board now and they can't take me back. I'm with my friends and we're going towards the shore together!

"Hey, Eddie! Did you see this crazy cat? She really wants to come with us! Silly kitty! I think you're making a big mistake." He pats my back as he's talking to me and I purr in response.

"Well, Mike, she's a brave little girl but this is pretty dangerous. Now guys! Keep your heads down. The enemy is going to start firing at us pretty soon!"

Sure enough, loud cannon noises mix with the noises from the boat engines. It sounds like a terrible thunder storm. I take a peek over the edge and see the shoreline light up at regular intervals. That must be our Navy's cannons firing on enemy positions.

Above our heads, our Allied fighter planes, called Spitfires, circle like hawks. A cloud of German planes is speeding toward them. Suddenly, our Spitfires open their machine guns and the airplanes fly off in every direction. Instead of flying in formation the planes are zooming everywhere, crossing paths with each other.

It's almost like a dance and could be beautiful if it wasn't so deadly.

All around us we hear boom, boom, booming. Enemy cannons are firing at us and sprays of water splash nearby.

"They're aiming at us! And we're not anywhere near the shoreline!" shouts Mike.

"Keep your heads down! Don't look overboard! You'll see your enemy soon enough!" yells the head officer.

Our little landing craft sways from side to side, making the soldiers fall to their knees. I lose my

balance, too. There are huge waves all around us from cannon shells exploding in the water.

The Allied boats are pitching and swirling like leaves in a wind storm.

I'm beginning to think coming along wasn't a great idea.

I decide to stay close to Mike and Eddie. They're hanging on to the side of the craft to keep from falling. Big splashes of water come over the side and everyone is soaking wet. Our boat sure seems a lot smaller out here in the open sea! This is certainly not a safe place for anybody, soldier or cat!

A huge crash knocks me down. The back of our boat has been hit! The engine fuel catches fire and pours across the floor.

The head officer yells out "Abandon ship! Right away! Abandon ship!"

Soldiers jump into the water and begin to swim away from the fire on our boat.

"Sorry kitty! You're going overboard too!" Hands grab me and suddenly I'm flying through the air.

"Miiaooooww!"

My claws are out and my paws are stretched out, but I can't fly.

I fall smack into the sea on my belly.

Cold saltwater fills my nose and mouth. It stings my eyes.

But without thinking, all four of my legs start to paddle and I hold my breath.

The surface seems far above me.

But soon I reach the top and swallow a huge gulp of air. I meow as loud as I can before a wave pushes me under. I can't see a thing but my legs are still moving. I'm fighting to reach the surface again.

Another breath, another meow, and then another wave. I go under once again. But this time I realize that I know how to swim. I wonder how that happened? No one has ever taught me!
But here I am, back at the surface and using my tail like a *rudder** to turn around in circles looking for help.

*a rudder is like a steering wheel on a car except that it is at the back of a boat and sticks down in the water, just like Spooky's tail

To the right, I see a soldier in the water and he's wearing a life jacket. If only he'll wait for me!

I meow as loud as I possibly can.

He looks back at me.

He hears me! He stops swimming and I catch up very quickly.

"I can't hold on to you, cat! You'll have to hang on however you can!"

His helmet has netting all over the top. The netting is usually for holding twigs and leaves as *camouflage*. Well, I figure that netting is good enough to hold a cat, too. I dig the claws on my forelegs into the netting and use my back legs to keep swimming. Off we go, headed for a landing craft, coming to rescue us.

*camouflage is a way of hiding something by changing the way it looks to resemble the surroundings

Pretty soon we're hauled aboard one of the *seaworthy* landing craft. In spite of the danger all around us, the sailors who drag us over the side have a sense of humor. They're teasing us as we collapse, exhausted onto the floor of the boat.

"Looks like you've got yourself a *stowaway!*"

My friendly Canadian has just enough strength left for a smile. As for me, I'm frozen and shivering so much that I can't move a whisker.

*seaworthy means a boat that can still float safely
*a stowaway is someone who is on board a boat but shouldn't be because they don't have a ticket

Someone tries to pry my feet off the soldier's head. The sailors see that I'm so cold that I cannot withdraw my claws. So, they simply take the helmet off the Canadian  and place it on the deck. My feet are still hooked in the netting. We're wrapped in woolen blankets, my Canadian friend, his helmet and me. He slides over closer to me and rubs my fur to help warm me up.

"You know, kitty, you were awfully brave out in the water. When I saw you swimming towards me with that determined look in your eye, I was afraid you'd scratch me to ribbons. But no, you are a smart cat. You knew that I could only help you out if you stayed calm. Good job, fur ball!"

His sing-song accent is comforting to me.

He seems like a nice young man. Very young, in fact. If I could speak, I'd ask him his age. He can't be much older than a teenager. Still, he called me a fur ball.

I must look terrible.

Little by little my paws begin to tingle as the blood flows back into them. I can move my toes and retract my claws. Finally, I can climb down off the helmet. Now, I just have to do a gigantic fur shake to rid myself of this awful salt water.

"Hey! You're getting me even wetter, cat! Knock it off!" he laughs.

But this feels *soooo* good that I must do it again, and again. I'm feeling a bit better now. More like a cat. So, I rub up against him to thank him for all he's done before settling down for a well-deserved bath. After all, cats are known for their cleanliness.

All around us men are being dragged from the sea, soaked and sometimes wounded. The news from the beach is bad. Things did not go as planned for the Allies. To save as many soldiers as possible, the call for retreat to England has been sent out. We're leaving, and fast.

Except, all of a sudden, the noise of an aerial combat reaches our ears. It's taking place directly overhead. A German fighter plane is chasing an Allied Spitfire, leaving behind a long trail of dark smoke. Another burst of gunfire from the German plane hits the side of the Allied plane. It begins to fall from the sky. Our eyes are glued to the battle above us. Luckily, the pilot has ejected and is floating gently down to sea in his parachute. A shout of joy echoes over the water.

"Let's go fellas! We have to reach him before something else happens to this poor guy!" The boat driver spins the wheel and our boat changes direction. We're off as fast as we can. "His parachute can drag him underwater if we don't hurry!"

When we reach the parachute, floating on the water like a giant jellyfish, no one can see the pilot. One of our soldiers stretches out his rifle to hook the soaking cloth of the parachute and haul it in. Everyone on board grabs a bit and pulls, searching for the man hidden underneath. I pull on a corner with my teeth.

A leather *aviator*'s hat appears in the folds of the cloth. The pilot blinks at us through his flight *goggles**.

He seems a little dizzy and confused. No wonder, after a fall like that!

"Climb aboard friend. You're safe now!

"Who are you?" asks the lieutenant, clearly a bit dazed. "...and where am I?"

*An aviator is someone who flies airplanes   *goggles are thick glasses set in a rubber frame to protect the eyes from wind

Well, listen to that! He's an American! Several of our soldiers grab him under the arms and hoist him over the side by his flight jacket. He slides onto the floor of the boat like a gigantic fish. I can help here. A few licks of my tongue will surely revive him.

"Ouch! Who's that wiping my face with sandpaper? You Canadian guys need to invest in softer towels!" Apparently, our pilot friend is doing fine.

"Here. Drink up and stop complaining. That's our ship's cat wishing you a warm welcome!" A hot cup of tea is placed in the pilot's hands which are blue and shaking with cold.

"...and this is for you, Mademoiselle Pussy Cat, some warm milk." A mug which smells absolutely wonderful appears beneath my nose. I take a deep breath. Yummmmm.

The American, with a blanket over his shoulders, turns to me and says "Here's to your health, Miss Ship's Kitty!"

The motor hums and we turn toward England and home.

The crossing takes a long time. Everyone has calmed down and is quiet. To one side of the deck two men are whispering about what they saw. I come closer to listen. I want to know what went wrong, too.

"What rotten luck! If those German boats hadn't seen our convoy coming, we could have surprised them. That's why we were crossing the English Channel at night, so they wouldn't see us!"

His friend replies, "Yeah, blast it all! You're right. And then all those German planes showed up, making it harder for our planes to help us out on the beach. And what about our tanks?"

"Yup, I saw that too. That beach was much too steep for our tanks to make it up the hill. They just got stuck at the bottom and couldn't shoot at any of the big German cannons." He hangs his head, frustrated.

"You know, sometimes it seems like everything just goes wrong. I think today was one of those days."

"I'm afraid you're right. I just hope the officers learned something from what happened today in Dieppe."

"Yeah, me too." They stop talking, both of them looking very sad.

The soldiers are most certainly thinking about what happened on the beach and about their friends who didn't get away. Some are probably taken prisoner. Some might be wounded. And some of them might be dead.

As I wander amongst the small groups of men sitting on the ground, sometimes I get a pat or two. Mostly, the atmosphere is very different from when we played on deck on the way over. Now, we understand what it's like to go into battle. We've met the enemy and we know that it isn't going to be easy to win this war against the Nazi army.

The sun is setting when we arrive safely in Newhaven, England. There's a lot of activity on the quay. It sounds like everyone is talking at the same time. There are so many questions, but no answers.

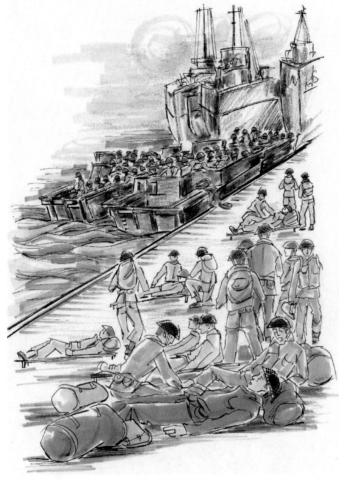

"Did you see Private Martin?"

"And what about Stevens? Didn't he get on your boat?"

"Is my friend, Fred with you guys?"

"I can't find my brother Michael. You didn't see what happened to him, did you?"

So many people lost! During roll call, there are terrible silences when no one answers. A red mark is placed next to the names of those missing in action. It's a very lost list with many, many red marks.

The officers have a lot of work to do. They go off to discuss what happened. There are important lessons to learn about what should be done next time and what should never be tried again.

The soldiers in the meantime, need to eat, rest and have their wounds tended. I have to get back to my job. The work of a good ship's cat is never over.

As I'm strolling back up the quay toward my ship, I hear footsteps coming up behind me.

"Hey, Cat! Spooky!" I recognize the sing-song voice of my Canadian swimming partner.

He scoops me up in his arms. "Stay here with me for a minute."

Some other Canadian soldiers, along with Mike and Eddie and the American pilot catch up to us.

My Canadian puts me down gently on the dock and kneels next to me.

"We have decided that you deserve a medal of honor for the way you behaved today, kitty. Here's a new collar that you can be proud to wear, Miss Spooky!" He fastens a silky red ribbon around my neck. On it hangs a beautiful bronze star.

He rises and takes a very serious pose. "For Miss Spooky, who showed courage and calm under fire." Then he snaps a salute. Just like the kind of salute a true military officer would get!

"Hip, Hip, Hurray!"

"Congratulations Miss Spooky!"

One by one the soldiers salute me before bending down to scratch my chin. I am purring as hard as I can, almost choking with pride and happiness. These brave young men risked their lives today. And they've honored me with a medal! Me, a ship's cat!

I know I will never forget this day. I know in my heart that sometime soon, we will work together as a team to kick Adolph Hitler's Nazi Army out of Europe. We can bring back peace to those who have lost it.

As for me, Spooky: Ship's Cat First Class, I'll be there
to help out!

Tails of War

Spooky: the Adventures of a Ship's cat in WWII, is inspired by the numerous animal recipients of the Dickin Medal of Honor for outstanding loyalty and service during times of war. Founded during the 2nd World War by Maria Dickin, the medal has been awarded to 4 horses, 28 dogs, 32 pigeons and a single cat.

Spooky's character is based on a cat by the name of Sooty, whose story differs somewhat from that told in this book. As this is historical fiction for young people, I've taken the liberty of adapting the conflicting versions of Sooty for the purposes of story-telling. Because this tale is written from Spooky's point of view, this was an obvious necessity. No one interviewed the cat.

I first read about Sooty at the Newhaven Fort Museum in England. I was charmed by the display of drawings and photos of a black and white feline. She was the only female of any species to actively participate in Operation Jubilee, as the infamous Raid on Dieppe was code-named. The soldiers accompanying her on the landing craft headed for the beach, spontaneously awarded her with one of their own medals. Thus, she is not the sole cat recipient of the Dickin Medal. His name was Simon. Still, Sooty's tale is an intruiging one.

I can only hope that those who read her story will be inspired to learn more about History via the individual anecdotes of those who are caught up in the making of it.

Made in the USA
Columbia, SC
13 May 2017